Betty Sydow

Carolou Nelson

The Adventures of
a Sparrow Named
Stanley

Written by
Betty Sydow

Illustrated by
Carolou Lennon Nelsen

Hidden Timber Books

Smash!

Crash!

Chirp!

Splash!

Who is making all that noise?

Can it be a lonely little bird?

This is the story of a young sparrow named Stanley who was just old enough to leave his mother's nest.

One sunny morning, Stanley's mother helped him pack his clothes and books, and they flew away together to find a nest of his own in the city. Stanley was a common house sparrow, and common house sparrows like to live in cities.

Stanley and his mother found a large oak tree with a hollowed-out space. The tree was in a grove, in a neighborhood with birdbaths and bird feeders. This would make a perfect home for a young sparrow, his mother thought.

Stanley's mother showed him how to gather dried grass, yarn, and twigs to make his nest comfortable. Then she flew home to her own nest.

Even though Stanley was now all alone, he felt very brave.

Stanley began to fix up his nest. Outside a laundromat, he found dryer lint for a soft, cozy bed. He smoothed out a crumpled piece of aluminum foil and tucked it on one wall of his nest for a mirror.

Stanley stood in front of the foil, puffing out his feathers to look strong and handsome. He squinted and pretended to be big, but it was no use. Stanley knew he was just a small sparrow, not a bird that other sparrows would notice.

After his nest was finished, Stanley felt lonely, for he had no friends to play with. As he wondered how he could make new friends, he heard loud music and flew off to investigate.

Stanley found a big parade marching down Main Street led by a red fire engine. He listened to the music. He saw a football player in an open top car. The football player smiled and waved at the crowd. People cheered and took his picture. Reporters held out microphones and asked him questions. Nobody noticed a little sparrow sitting in the tree. Stanley wanted to be noticed!

Stanley asked himself, "How can I become famous, so other sparrows will want to be my friends?"

Stanley knew he could not be a football player, so he would have to find another way to be famous. But what could he do? He was just a common house sparrow.

The next day, as Stanley flew around his neighborhood, he heard lovely bird songs coming from an open window. Stanley flew to the window ledge where he saw a canary sitting on a perch, singing joyfully. A young girl entered the room. She took the canary out of his cage, stroked his feathers, and talked to him.

"What a good bird you are," she said. "Your songs are so happy. Everyone loves you."

Before leaving the room, the girl filled the canary's water bowl and added seeds to his dish. She never noticed a little sparrow sitting outside the window.

The canary began singing again, so Stanley rapped his beak on the window, peered under the sash, and asked the canary, "How did you learn to sing like that?"

"This is what canaries do," the bird said. "I just open my beak and think happy thoughts."

Stanley wondered if he could sing like a canary, then he might be famous and make many friends.

tanley sat on the window ledge all morning trying to sing trills and chirps like the canary. But all he could manage were squawks and harsh rattles until his throat was very sore.

Stanley flew home and gargled with salt water. He could not talk for three days and three nights. He told himself, "I don't want to live locked up in a cage, anyway."

But Stanley still wanted to be famous. Maybe if he flew to the countryside, he would find an idea.

In the countryside, Stanley spotted several loons swimming in a lake. The loons were splashing and diving under water only to pop up far from where he expected.

Stanley sat in the shade of an old barn near a group of children who were laughing and shouting to each other.

"Look at these silly loons! Aren't they wonderful!" the children said. The children tried to guess where the loons would come up out of the water, but the loons always surprised them. The children never noticed a little sparrow sitting in the shadows.

After the children left, Stanley said to the loon, "That looks like great fun. How did you learn to swim like that?"

"That's what we do," the loon said. "I just hold my breath, dive down deep, and swim away."

With that, the loon dived and was gone.

Stanley thought this trick could make him famous, but he knew Loon Lake was too large for him to practice splashing and diving. He found a child's swimming pool where he tried again and again to dive like the loons, but he could not hold his breath long enough. Stanley sputtered and choked and got soaking wet until he had to stop.

He dried his feathers at home and went to bed to rest for three days and three nights.

"Never mind," Stanley said to himself. "I don't want to be wet all the time. I need to think of something really different. What can it be?"

A few nights later, just as he was about to fall asleep, he heard bats swooping past his tree. Stanley thought that it must be wonderful to fly at night. No house sparrows can do that.

He wondered aloud, "How can bats see when it is so dark? If I could do that, I would be as famous as a football player!!" Before he fell asleep, he thought of an exciting plan.

The next day, Stanley took a long afternoon nap to be ready for his big adventure. When he heard bats flying outside his nest early that evening, he called out and asked how they fly in the dark.

"It is easy for bats," one said, speaking fast as he swooped in circles around Stanley. "We don't use our eyes. We listen for echoes that bounce off trees and houses." The bat flew past Stanley again. "Then we fly around them."

The bat disappeared into the dark to catch mosquitoes for his dinner.

Stanley ruffled his feathers and stretched his wings. He was ready.

He took a running start, trying to miss trees and houses by humming as he flew, but he heard no echoes. He bumped his head and crashed down to the ground until he was bruised and his feet were sore. He sat on a branch until daylight when he could see again.

In the morning, nobody noticed a tired little sparrow flying sadly home.

Stanley covered his head and feet with bandages, then went to bed for three days and three nights.

"Who cares," he whispered. "I don't want to eat mosquitoes all night anyway."

Stanley needed expert advice. But where could he find it? He remembered his mother telling him that owls were the wisest birds.

Because owls sleep all day and hunt for food at night, Stanley looked for an owl at sunset.

One evening he saw a pair of bright yellow eyes high in a tree top. The eyes belonged to a great gray owl, the largest owl in the land. Stanley sat near the owl, but not too near, for he didn't know if the owl wanted a sparrow for his dinner.

Stanley asked, "Are you a friendly owl?"

"I can be," the owl replied. So Stanley moved closer to tell the owl how he tried to be famous but nothing worked. Stanley asked the wise owl to help him. The owl thought for a minute, then asked, "Why do you want to be famous?"

Stanley answered right away, "So lots of sparrows will know about me and be my friends."

The owl told him, "Stop trying to imitate others. Be the best sparrow you can be."

"But how will that help me make friends?" Stanley asked.

"Think about why friends like to be together," the owl said. He stared at Stanley, blinked once, then repeated, "Be the best sparrow you can be."

Stanley watched the owl fly down, scoop up a field mouse, and carry it away to feed his baby owls. I'm glad I was careful not to sit too close, Stanley thought.

The next morning Stanley flew off to find some other young sparrows. He met a group of sparrows tumbling about, having fun.

"What are you doing?" Stanley asked.

"We want to be in the Bird Olympics next year," they said. "So we are practicing to be strong, but that is hard to do outside when it is raining or snowing."

Here was Stanley's chance to make friends. "I'd like to do that, too," he said. Then he added, "Can I join you? I have an idea."

He took them to a gym where people exercise. When they saw all the machines, the sparrows were amazed.

"We can build our own sparrow-sized machines," Stanley said. "People throw away a lot of good items. We can go to junk yards and dumpsters." He continued, "I think I know of a building for our machines, too."

He told them about the old empty barn at Loon Lake. Stanley led them to that spot and asked the loons if the sparrows could fix up the barn and use it for a gym. The loons said yes, and all the sparrows agreed to work together.

It was hard work, but they had fun. Stanley was a good leader. He painted signs that read, "Stanley's Gym for Young Sparrows–Opening Soon."

Stanley added a bicycle, a treadmill, a leg press machine, and a wing press machine. He started classes in healthy eating and yoga. All the young sparrows worked hard, and they took turns sharing the machines.

Some of the sparrows did win medals in the Bird Olympics, and all of the sparrows were happy being together.

Stanley's mother came to the gym's Grand Opening Party. She was proud of Stanley and happy to meet his friends.

As time passed and news of his gym traveled across the land, many more Stanley's Gyms for Young Sparrows opened.

Stanley remembered what the wise old owl told him, and hung another sign in the front entrance of each gym:

Be the Best Sparrow You Can Be.

Many people helped turn Stanley's story into this book.
Special thanks to Christi Craig, Lisa Rivero, Mary Day Lewis,
LaVerne Ferguson, Eleanor Hoehn and the
Harwood Bucket List Project.

Text copyright © 2016 by Betty Sydow
Illustrations copyright © 2016 by Carolou Lennon Nelsen
All rights reserved.

Hidden Timber Books
Milwaukee, WI
www.hiddentimberbooks.com/stanley

ISBN 978-0-9906530-0-4 (paperback) – ISBN 978-0-9906530-1-1 (hardcover)
Library of Congress Control Number: 2016935234
The Adventures of a Sparrow Named Stanley / written by Betty Sydow; illustrated
by Carolou Lennon Nelsen

Summary: Stanley is a little sparrow who wants to be noticed, but in his attempts
to be famous, he learns about something much more important.

The illustrations are rendered in watercolor pencil.

The Adventures of Betty and Carolou

Author Betty Sydow grew up and has spent most of her life in the Milwaukee area, enjoying camping, swimming, sailing, and racquetball. After retiring from a 30-year nursing career, she stumbled upon a creative writing class and was hooked. The story of Stanley began as a fable but over a year's time grew into a children's book. She asked her artist friend Carolou if she would illustrate Stanley's story, and, months later, Stanley came alive between the covers of this book.

Illustrator Carolou Lennon Nelsen grew up in Oak Park, Illinois, and spent most of her adult life in the Milwaukee area. She has worked as an art educator, raised two children, and has a master's degree in social work. When her friend Betty Sydow asked her to illustrate her picture book about Stanley the sparrow, she was immediately drawn to its message of the strength of individuality.

Betty Sydow (standing) & Carolou Lennon Nelsen
Photo credit: Amy Bielawski

CPSIA information can be obtained at www.ICGtesting.com
Printed in the USA
LVIW01n2150090516
487467LV00011B/22